SOFTBALL
Switch-Up

BY JAKE MADDOX

text by Natasha Deen
illustrated by Katie Wood

STONE ARCH BOOKS
a capstone imprint

Jake Maddox Girl Sports Stories are published by Stone Arch Books
a Capstone imprint
1710 Roe Crest Drive
North Mankato, Minnesota 56003
www.capstonepub.com

Text and illustrations © 2020 Stone Arch Books.

Library of Congress Cataloging-in-Publication Data
Names: Maddox, Jake, author. | Deen, Natasha, author. | Wood, Katie,
1981– illustrator. | Maddox, Jake. Jake Maddox girl sports stories.
Title: Softball switch-up / by Jake Maddox ; text by Natasha Deen ;
illustrated by Katie Wood.
Description: North Mankato, Minnesota : an imprint of Stone Arch
Books, [2019] | Series: Jake Maddox. Jake Maddox girls sports stories |
Summary: When the coach of her championship softball team asks Raisa
Kumar to teach a new recruit, Annie, how to pitch, Raisa is eager to help,
especially since she hopes to be a coach herself someday; but when the
team's other pitcher turns up with a broken arm, teaching Annie takes
on a new urgency—and Raisa's efforts at coaching seem to be frustrating
Annie rather than helping her.
Identifiers: LCCN 2019000271 | ISBN 9781496583246 (hardcover) |
ISBN 9781496584502 (pbk.) | ISBN 9781496583260 (ebook pdf)
Subjects: LCSH: Softball—Juvenile fiction. | Pitching (Softball)—Juvenile
fiction. | Coaching (Athletics)—Juvenile fiction. | Teamwork (Sports)—
Juvenile fiction. | Self-confidence—Juvenile fiction. | CYAC: Softball—
Fiction. | Coaching (Athletics)—Fiction. | Teamwork (Sports)—Fiction. |
Self-confidence—Fiction. | East Indian Americans—Fiction.
Classification: LCC PZ7.M25643 Sop 2019 | DDC 813.6 [Fic]—dc23
LC record available at https://lccn.loc.gov/2019000271

Designer: Tracy McCabe
Production Specialist: Katy LaVigne
Design Elements: Shutterstock

Printed and bound in the USA.
PA70

TABLE OF CONTENTS

CHAPTER 1

Stepping Up for the Team

Raisa Kumar was in her room, dusting the softball trophy on her shelf. The new season started on Tuesday. She was excited to reunite with her team, the Tigers. Raisa paused as she heard her grandmother's voice.

"Raisa!" Nona called. "There's someone here to see you."

"Coming!" Raisa ran to the kitchen. Coach Garcia, her softball team's head coach, was sitting at the table.

Why is Coach Garcia here? she wondered. *I hope everything is OK.*

"Hello, Raisa," the coach said. She pointed at the dust cloth in Raisa's hand. "Were you cleaning?"

Raisa blushed. "Dusting my softball trophy," she said.

Nona laughed. "You dust it every day! Keep it up, and you'll wear a hole in it!" she joked.

"I can't help it!" Raisa said. "We won our first championship last season. I want us to win again."

Coach Garcia smiled. "I'm glad you're proud. Your pitching was one of the reasons we beat out fifteen other teams." She leaned forward. "In fact, your pitching is why I'm here."

Raisa's stomach fluttered. She was the team's starting pitcher.

Did I mess something up? I hope she's not here to tell me she's moving me, she thought nervously.

"I wanted to talk to you about our new player: Annie Nanton," Coach Garcia said. "She's new to the game. I'm starting her out in right field, but she's eager to learn how to pitch too."

Raisa blew out a relieved breath. "Fantastic!" she said. "It's just me and Kaitlyn pitching now. An extra person would be great."

"Exactly," Coach Garcia said with a smile. "Would you like to help Annie learn how to pitch?" She winked. "I know you want to be a coach one day. This might be good practice."

Raisa's stomach fluttered again, but this time from happiness. "Yes, please!" she exclaimed. "I'll help her outside of our team practices."

"Wonderful," Coach Garcia said. "With your help, Annie's going to have a lot of fun learning how to pitch. I'll text you her number and let her know she can expect to hear from you." She stood. "I'll see you at practice on Tuesday. Thanks for being there for her."

Raisa nodded. She was already thinking of the drills she could teach Annie. Together they'd take the Tigers to their second championship win.

CHAPTER 2

Sharing the Mound

After Coach Garcia left, Raisa texted Annie.

Raisa: *Hi, Annie! I'm Raisa! Welcome to the Tigers!*

Annie: *Hi! Thanks. ^_^*

Raisa: *I'm the starting pitcher for the team. Coach Garcia said you want to pitch too. I'd love to help you!*

Annie: *That's Gr8 news! TY! Do you want to start today?*

Raisa: *Sure! Do you want to meet some of the team? Julia, Kaitlyn, and Taylor are super nice. Kaitlyn is a pitcher too.*

Annie: *That would be Gr8! TY!* :D

Raisa started a new group text to her friends, then added Annie.

Raisa: *Hi, guys! Meet Annie. She's new to the Tigers. Want to meet up at the park today @ 1 to practice?*

Julia: *Definitely!*

Kaitlyn: *Can't wait to meet you in person, Annie.*

Taylor: *Me too! C U soon!!*

Raisa held her phone to her chest. *I'm already helping the team!* she thought proudly. *This is going to be the best season ever!*

* * *

After she finished eating lunch, Raisa told her grandmother she was headed to meet her friends, then biked to the nearby softball field. She sat on the bench and waited for everyone.

A few moments later, a redheaded girl carrying a softball mitt approached her. "Are you Raisa?" the girl asked.

Raisa smiled. "Annie?"

The girl grinned. "Yep!" she replied.

As she stood up, Raisa noticed Annie was much shorter than she was. In fact, she was shorter than most of the pitchers Raisa knew. But she didn't think that would matter when it came to pitching.

Just then, Julia and Taylor arrived.

"Hi!" the blond girl said, waving at Annie. "I'm Taylor!"

Julia tucked her braids into her cap. "And I'm Julia," she added.

"Hi," Annie replied with a shy smile. "Thanks for meeting up with me. I was so nervous to move here from Wisconsin! I'm excited to be on the team. This is my first year in softball."

"You're going to love being a part of the Tigers," Taylor said.

"I hope so!" Annie replied. "My grandma used to be a pitcher, and she made it sound so fun. I can't wait to try it."

"Where's Kaitlyn?" Raisa asked as they began stretching. She looked around for the other pitcher.

"She's probably just running late," said Taylor. "She can catch up when she gets here."

Raisa nodded. After they finished stretching, they ran laps. Then Raisa handed Annie one of the softballs she'd brought with her.

"Let's start with the grip," she said. "See how this seam looks like a horseshoe? Put your index and middle fingers here, and then put your thumb here." Raisa demonstrated how to grip the ball.

Annie mimicked Raisa. "Like this?" she asked.

"That's a good start," Raisa said. She adjusted Annie's grip. "How does that feel?"

"Weird. I've seen photos of my grandma, and she held the ball like this." Annie moved her fingers so she held the ball with a four-finger grip instead of three. "Can I do that?"

Raisa shook her head. "That's a grip for more experienced pitchers," she said. "Since you're new, you'll want to hold it with three fingers."

Annie nodded and readjusted her grip on the ball.

"Let me show you how to throw," Raisa offered. She motioned to her friends, and Taylor stepped up to bat. Julia, the team's catcher, crouched behind Taylor.

Raisa turned to Annie. "Watch me." She rotated her left arm into a windmill motion and sent a pitch Taylor's way. Taylor hit the ball back to her. The next time, Raisa snapped her wrist as she released the ball. This made the ball go faster. Taylor swung and missed. Julia caught the ball and tossed it back.

"Can I try?" Annie asked.

Raisa didn't want to give up the mound. *But a good coach—and teammate—would give Annie a chance,* she thought.

Raisa handed over the ball. Annie threw it to Julia. It sailed high and came down to the outside of home plate, outside the strike zone.

"That's a ball," Raisa said. "But you were close to home plate. It's a great start!"

Julia held the bat out to Annie. "Let's see what you've got!" she said.

Annie stepped to the plate. Raisa pitched the ball to her, and Annie hit it with a solid *crack!* It sailed over Raisa's head and toward second base. Taylor ran to catch it.

"Wow!" Julia said. "You're a great hitter!"

"If you keep batting like that we're going to win every game, including the championship!" Taylor cheered.

"Thanks," Annie said, blushing. "I hope you're right. But this is my first year. I still have a lot to learn."

Raisa turned as a car pulled into the lot. "There's Kaitlyn. Finally!" she exclaimed.

But when Kaitlyn climbed out of the car, the other girls gasped. Kaitlyn's right arm was in a cast.

"Kaitlyn!" Raisa said as the other pitcher walked closer. "What happened?"

"I slipped and fell coming down the stairs," Kaitlyn said as she came closer. "I broke my arm." There were tears in her brown eyes. "I can come to practice, but I can't play until the cast comes off."

A surge of anger ran through Raisa. Kaitlyn's broken arm meant they were down a pitcher. That wasn't going to help their chances of winning another championship.

It's not Kaitlyn's fault she broke her arm, Raisa told herself. But she couldn't fully shake her irritation.

"But we need you!" Julia cried. "The league rules say a pitcher can only pitch four innings max. With you out, Annie will have to take the mound."

"Four innings! But I'm new!" Annie exclaimed.

"It'll be fine," Raisa said. But truthfully, she was worried too. *What if I don't have what it takes to coach Annie?* she thought. *What if I cost us the championship? I can't let my friends down.*

Raisa forced a bright smile. "With my help, you'll be a great pitcher *and* help the team win our games! I promise!"

CHAPTER 3

The Pitcher Goes Wild

On Tuesday, Nona drove Raisa to practice. *The team is counting on me,* Raisa reminded herself. *I have to help Annie.*

Coach Garcia waved everyone in. She handed out uniforms, and the girls pulled the orange-and-blue jerseys over their heads.

"A few of you have already met her," Coach Garcia began, "but I'd like to introduce our newest player, Annie."

Annie waved, and the team cheered for her.

Coach Garcia led the team through their warm-up. She hit grounders to the infield and fly balls to the outfield to get everyone's muscles loosened. Then, while the rest of the players started batting practice with the assistant coach, Coach Garcia pulled Raisa, Julia, and Annie aside for pitching drills.

Julia stood at the backstop and held her mitt out as a target for the ball. Kaitlyn watched from the side.

"You're right-handed, Annie," Coach Garcia said as she walked to the mound with Raisa and Annie. "So start with your right foot here."

Coach Garcia tapped the rubber plate on the ground with her toe. Then she held her hands straight out in front of her. The ball was in her right hand, and her mitt was in her left.

Coach Garcia swung her right hand up and around, in a windmill motion. She pushed off with her feet and pitched the ball to Julia. It landed in Julia's mitt with a loud *smack!*

"Go ahead and give it a try," Coach Garcia said. She stood back as Julia tossed the ball to Annie.

Annie stepped to the mound. Instead of keeping her right arm in front of her and rotating up, as the coach had done, Annie swung her hand behind her, then swung it back to the front.

Annie threw the ball, but it went wild. Julia dived to catch it.

She's not doing it right, Raisa thought with a frown. *Maybe Coach will correct her.*

But Coach Garcia just called, "Nice try!"

Raisa's frown deepened. *Didn't she see Annie miss the target?* she wondered. *Maybe this is one of the things she's counting on me to help with.*

"Try again," said Coach Garcia.

Annie nodded and threw the ball again, but this time her pitch was too soft. The ball landed a few feet from Julia. She scrambled to grab it.

She's still learning, Raisa told herself. *It's just the first practice.*

But she felt impatient. If they were going to win, Annie needed to learn—fast.

The next time, Annie tossed the ball harder. It was another wild pitch. Julia jumped backward to catch it.

"Keep trying. That's what counts," Coach Garcia told Annie.

Raisa blew out a tight breath. *I know Coach Garcia has to be encouraging,* she thought, *but we need a solid pitcher. I'll have to help Annie learn to pitch like me on our own time.*

After thirty minutes of pitching practice, it was time to join the team for batting drills.

"You'll have to practice with Annie," Kaitlyn said, echoing Raisa's thoughts. "Otherwise we'll never win."

"Maybe we can both help her," Raisa said. *If Kaitlyn helps, it won't be as much pressure on me,* she thought privately.

"You have to do it, Raisa. You're the starting pitcher," Julia said, overhearing their conversation.

Raisa didn't want to let her teammates down. She nodded. "You're right," she said. "Consider it handled."

"Annie, you're up to bat!" Coach called.

Annie stepped up to the batting tee and swung. Her bat connected, and the ball sailed to second base.

Raisa cheered. Annie was a great hitter. She just needed help pitching, and it was up to Raisa to teach her.

CHAPTER 4

Annie Strikes Out

A few days later it was time for the Tigers' first game of the season against the Meteors. *I hope all the practicing Annie and I have been doing pays off,* Raisa thought as she and Nona parked.

After they'd walked to the field, Nona gave Raisa a hug. "Good luck! Have fun!" she said.

Raisa smiled and relaxed a little. Softball was always fun—there was no question about that.

After Coach Garcia went through the batting order and lineup with the team, Raisa took her place on the mound. The Meteors' player got into position, and Raisa let the ball fly.

* * *

A few innings later, the score was 3–1, Tigers. Raisa wanted to make sure it stayed that way. There was already one out on the board.

Raisa ground the ball into her glove and threw a fastball. The ball sailed past the Meteors' player and into Julia's catcher's mitt.

"Strike three!" the umpire called.

The next player stepped up to the plate. Raisa pitched and snapped her wrist as she released the ball.

The player swung, and the tip of her bat caught the edge of the ball. It sailed high and short. Raisa raced under it and grinned as the solid weight of the ball landed in her glove.

"Out!" the umpire called. "Batters up!"

That was the signal to switch. Raisa followed her teammates to the bench for their turn at bat.

Annie was up first. Thinking about what was on the line for the team, Raisa grabbed her new friend's arm.

"Remember to bend at the knees," Raisa said. "When you hit the ball, follow through with your hips. We're counting on you."

Annie's face whitened, but she nodded. She gripped the bat and got into position. The pitcher tossed the ball, and Annie swung.

"Strike one!" the umpire yelled.

"The next one's yours!" Raisa shouted.

But the next pitch was a swing and a miss. "Strike two!" the umpire called.

"Come on," muttered Taylor. "She's going to cost us the game."

"She's trying," Raisa snapped.

But it wasn't enough. A moment later, the umpire declared, "Strike three!"

Annie shuffled back to the dugout.

"It's OK," Raisa said, sensing that Annie needed encouragement. "We all have bad moments."

Annie didn't say anything.

* * *

When it was time to switch, the Tigers were still ahead. It was Annie's turn on the mound.

"Do I have to pitch?" Annie asked. "I'm not good enough yet."

"Raisa can't pitch more than four innings—league rules," Coach Garcia reminded her.

Raisa smiled. "You'll do great. Just do it like me."

Annie nodded and ran to the mound.

"I hope she doesn't mess up," Julia said quietly as she put on her catcher's mask.

"She'll be fine," Raisa said tightly.

But three batters later, she was having trouble believing her own words. Even though Annie was pitching just like Raisa did, it wasn't going well. All three batters had made it on base.

Annie threw the ball again, but instead of heading straight to the plate, it veered left.

"Ball!" the umpire called.

Annie glowered, took a breath, and threw the ball again. This time it crossed the edge of the plate. The Meteors' batter smashed it far into right field.

"We're doomed," Taylor muttered from her spot on the bench.

"Give her a chance," Raisa said.

But by the time the game was done, Annie had had more than enough chances. The Tigers had not only lost their lead, they'd lost the game, 5–3.

CHAPTER 5

Practice Doesn't Make Perfect

After the game, no one felt like hanging out. That night, Raisa texted Annie. They agreed to meet at the park the next day.

"I feel terrible," Annie said when she arrived. "I lost the game for us."

Raisa said, "You met me today for practice. You're working hard. That matters more than one bad game."

Annie nodded but seemed unconvinced.

They warmed up quickly. Then Raisa pulled on her glove and squatted behind home plate.

"Throw the ball to where my mitt is," she said. She positioned it in front of her chest.

Annie tried, but the ball went wide.

She's still learning, Raisa reminded herself. *Be patient.*

"You're swinging your arm back before you swing it forward," Raisa said. "That's not how I do it. You shouldn't, either. Plus, you're not getting enough power. Look at how you're planting your feet." She showed Annie how to take the stance. "Do it just like how I do it."

"My feet feel too far away from each other," Annie argued, closing her stance. "I like it this way."

"You're new to pitching." Raisa felt her patience slipping. "It'll feel weird until you get used to it. This is what works for me and Kaitlyn. I know it will work for you too." She punched her glove. "Come on, put one in."

Annie sighed and pitched again. This time, the ball landed on target.

"See! What did I tell you?" Raisa exclaimed. She tossed the ball back.

Annie scowled. "It feels uncomfortable," she argued. She shifted so her legs were closer together. "This feels better."

"It's not right," Raisa told her firmly.

"But Coach Garcia—" Annie started.

"The Tigers have a chance to win a second championship," Raisa said. "But only if we pitch well. The team is counting on us. Don't you want to be a team player?"

"I do!" Annie said. "I'll try harder."

Raisa threw the ball to her. "Try it, just like I showed you, three more times," she called. "Widen your stance! Push off with your lead foot! Dig your foot in!"

Annie tried to follow Raisa's instructions, but her tosses were wild and off target. "This isn't working," she said.

She's not trying hard enough, Raisa thought, swallowing her frustration. "Do it like I showed you, and you'll be fine," she said.

Annie scowled but tried again.

"You're not getting enough speed and power in your throws," Raisa said. "Let's try the windmill motion together."

Annie's mouth pressed into a hard line, but she nodded.

* * *

All week, Annie and Raisa met to practice. Sometimes Julia, Kaitlyn, and Taylor met up to watch.

"She's totally hopeless," Julia said as they watched Annie throw balls at the target. "You'd think with all of this practice, she'd be getting better, but somehow she's getting worse."

Taylor folded her arms. "Our next game is against the Sharks, and if she pitches like this, we're going to lose," she said. "Raisa, you should talk to Coach."

"Maybe she should try pitching the way Coach Garcia showed her," Kaitlyn suggested.

Raisa shook her head. "You and I have the same pitching style. That's what won us a championship," she said. "We just have to be patient. She'll get it."

But truthfully, Raisa was as frustrated as her friends. She wanted Annie to have a chance to prove she could be a great pitcher. And Raisa wanted to prove she was a great coach.

Why can't she just put more power and speed into her pitches? Raisa thought.

As they watched, Annie sent another wild pitch to the right of the target. Julia chased it down and tossed the ball back, but shot Raisa an I-told-you-so look.

"Taylor's right," Julia said when she returned. "Raisa, you need to talk to Coach and tell her Annie shouldn't be pitching."

Just then, Annie squealed. "I got it! I hit the target!"

Raisa clapped, but she felt terrible. Her friends were right. *Annie isn't a great pitcher,* she thought, *but how do I tell her that?*

CHAPTER 6

Curveball

Later that week, when Raisa arrived for the game against the Sharks, Annie was already there.

This is my chance, Raisa thought. She ran up to give her friend some last-minute advice.

"Remember what we practiced," Raisa said. "Keep your hips square, widen your stance, make sure you really push off the mound—"

"I know," Annie said, "You've told me a thousand times."

Raisa placed her hand on Annie's shoulder. "The team is counting on you. Remember?" she said. "We're going to win the championship—together. But we have to win here first."

Annie pulled away. "I have to warm up," she snapped.

Why can't Annie see I'm trying to help? Raisa thought. *If she doesn't listen, we'll lose the game. The whole team will be mad at her—and me. I can't let that happen.*

The Tigers were up to bat first. Julia hit the ball far into left field and made it to second base. Taylor was next to the plate. She hit the ball to right field and raced to first base while Julia sped toward third.

Then it was Raisa's turn. Her bat connected firmly with the ball, sending it flying to center field.

Julia and Taylor made it home, scoring two runs. Raisa made it to second base.

Raisa clapped as Annie stepped to the plate. "Bring me home!" she shouted.

The pitcher threw the ball, and Annie connected! She dropped the bat and ran, but the first baseman caught the ball. Annie was out, but the Tigers were still ahead. At the end of the second inning, the score was 2–0.

Raisa stepped to the mound. She had to maintain their lead, for Annie and the team. The Tigers had to win today. Raisa threw the ball. It whizzed past the batter.

"Strike one!" the umpire called.

Raisa relaxed her shoulders. She threw out another pitch.

"Strike two!" the umpire shouted.

One more throw, and Raisa struck out the first batter. The next player struck out too, but the one after that made it to second base.

Coach Garcia called Raisa off the mound.

"I can keep going," Raisa said.

Pitching felt great, but winning would feel even better. If she stayed on the mound, she could help the team *and* take the pressure off of Annie.

Isn't that what a coach is supposed to do? Raisa thought. *Help everyone?*

"You know the rules," Coach Garcia told her. "It's Annie's turn. You have to share the mound."

As Raisa made her way to the dugout, she noticed Annie was holding the ball with a four-finger grip instead of a three-finger grip.

"Check your grip," Raisa whispered, but Annie ignored her.

Raisa bit the inside of her cheek so she wouldn't yell at Annie, but she was angry. She was doing all she could to help the team.

Why isn't Annie doing her share? Raisa thought.

The batter walked to the plate. Annie threw the ball, but she didn't push off the mound in the way Raisa would have. The batter easily hit the ball and sent it into left field. While the Tigers scrambled to catch the ball, the batter made it to third.

Raisa held her breath as Annie threw the ball to the next batter. The Sharks' player hit it into the outfield and ran to first base. The player on third base made it home. The score was tied 2–2.

Raisa's anger rose. Annie was ignoring all their hard work. Worse, she was giving the Sharks a chance to win.

For the rest of her time on the mound, Annie pitched the way she wanted. No surprise, the Tigers lost the game.

"You have to talk to Coach," Taylor said to Raisa after the game. "Annie just cost us a win." She ran to meet her parents.

Raisa knew she needed to talk to the coach, but first she had to talk to Annie.

"Our next game is against the Jets, and they're the best in the league," Raisa said as she approached Annie. "If you don't pitch like I taught you, we'll never win." Raisa tried not to sound angry, but she couldn't help it. "What were you doing out there today?"

"Playing the game," Annie said.

"Not like I taught you," Raisa told her.

Annie shoved her glove into her bag. "You didn't *teach* me anything! All you've done is *tell* me. Tell me how to pitch and how to stand. You haven't even tried to listen to me! You just force me to do it your way, and I hate it!"

Raisa stared at her in shock as Annie zipped up her bag. "You keep talking about how I need to be a good team player, but what about you?" Annie continued. "I just wanted to learn how to pitch and have fun with my new team. You ruined everything!"

With that, Annie slung her bag over her shoulder and stalked away. Raisa stared after her. How had this all gone so wrong? She needed to talk to Coach Garcia.

CHAPTER 7

A Sudden Realization

The next day, Raisa texted Coach Garcia to see if she could stop by. Then she asked Nona to drive her to the coach's house.

When Raisa arrived, Coach Garcia was in her garage, rummaging through the shelves.

"Hi, Raisa," she said. "I have an old playbook in here somewhere. I wish I knew where I'd hidden it!"

Raisa wasn't sure how to tell Coach Garcia about her frustrations. Instead she said, "Can I help you look for it?"

"Thank you!" Coach Garcia replied. "It's a blue binder. It might be in one of these boxes." The coach pointed to a set of boxes high on the shelf. "What did you want to talk about?"

I don't want Coach to think I'm not up for helping Annie, Raisa thought. *And I don't want to get Annie in trouble for not being a team player. . . .*

"I think Annie's having a hard time," she said. "She's trying, but her pitches aren't as fast or powerful as mine. I think she's frustrated."

"I don't blame her," Coach Garcia said.

Raisa glanced at her coach in surprise. That wasn't the answer she'd been expecting.

"You don't?" Raisa asked. She took a box off the shelf and handed it to her coach.

Coach Garcia shook her head and said, "Annie is much shorter than you. You're tall, so your arms and legs are longer. It's easier for you to throw the ball hard and get real power in your pitches. I noticed Annie tries to stand and pitch just like you. That has to be hard, given the height difference."

The coach paused for a moment. "She must really look up to you. In practice, she pitches the way I coach her, but at the games, it's all Raisa-style. No matter how much we talk about it, she won't stop imitating you."

Raisa groaned. "What's wrong?" the coach asked.

Raisa knew she needed to come clean about why she'd come to the coach's house. *But what if Coach is upset with me?* she worried. *What if* everyone *is?*

"I came to talk to you about Annie not listening to me," Raisa said. "I told her to pitch like me, because my way helped win the championship. I wanted us to win it again. Everyone does."

Coach Garcia sighed. "I wondered what the problem was," she said.

Raisa looked down. *I have to be honest,* she thought. *I have to tell Coach everything.*

"I'm the problem," Raisa confessed. "Annie kept telling me my way wasn't working, but I ignored her. I didn't think about how our height difference could affect how Annie pitched. I feel terrible. No wonder she's mad at me."

Coach Garcia put her hand on Raisa's shoulder. "No," she said, "you've been human. It's OK to make mistakes. The important thing is that you realized it."

Coach's smile made Raisa feel a little better. "I need to apologize to her," Raisa said. "Then see if she'll give me a chance to keep helping her."

Coach Garcia smiled. "That's a great idea," she agreed. "Why don't you text Annie and see if she wants to come here and talk?"

Raisa took out her phone and texted Annie: *Hey, it's me . . . can we talk? I'm at Coach Garcia's house. She says you can come over here.*

Annie wrote back right away: *I was hoping you would text! I was just going to text you too! I'll get my dad to drive me over right now.*

Raisa put her phone back in her pocket and blew out an anxious breath. She hoped Annie would give her another chance to be teammates and friends.

* * *

"I'm sorry," Raisa blurted out as soon as Annie arrived. "I was talking to Coach Garcia, and I realized what a jerk I've been." She held her breath and waited to see if Annie would forgive her.

"No," Annie said. "I was the one who was wrong. You were trying to help. I was frustrated, and I took it out on you. Please don't give up on me. I'll do what you say, I promise."

Raisa grabbed her friend's hand. "No! I mean, yes," she corrected. "Of course, I'll help you. But I'm part of the reason you were frustrated. Coach explained that because you're smaller than me, it's harder for you to get the kind of speed and power I get in my pitches. It's probably also why it feels better when you hold the ball with a four-finger grip instead of three fingers."

"Really?" Annie said.

Raisa nodded. "I'm sorry I didn't listen when you tried to tell me that. If you let me, I promise this time I'll coach you in a way that actually helps you."

Annie grinned. "Let's get started!"

Coach Garcia, Raisa, and Annie collected gloves, a bat, and a few balls, then headed to the field behind the coach's house.

Annie adjusted her stance so her legs were closer together and switched her grip to four fingers instead of three.

"Go ahead," Raisa crouched down. "Send one to me."

Annie spun her arm and sent the fastball Raisa's way. The ball smacked into her mitt.

"Wow! That was awesome!" Raisa stood.

"It's easier to push off hard when my legs are closer together. And it's easier to spin my arm because I have better balance," Annie said.

"It shows! The pitch had a lot more power and speed. Great job, girls!" Coach Garcia said.

Annie grinned. "Wait until the Jets get a load of us!" she cheered.

CHAPTER 8

What's Best for the Team

"What is she doing?" Taylor asked. She pointed at Annie, who was warming up her pitching arm. "You promised to talk to Coach Garcia."

Kaitlyn and Julia joined them at that moment. Julia nodded at the other team. "Taylor is right," she agreed. "We're playing the Jets. We need to play our best. You have to do the right thing for the whole team."

Raisa's heart raced at the thought of arguing with her friends. But she knew what she had to say.

"That's what I'm doing," she said. "I'm helping Annie become a better player." She took a breath. "None of us were great when we started. Where would we be if Coach Garcia hadn't let us play because she was worried we wouldn't win a trophy?"

Kaitlyn blushed. Julia stared at her feet.

"I want to win another championship too," Raisa said. "But what's the point of winning anything if we're always mad at each other? Being together and playing as a team *is* what's best for the team."

Kaitlyn shuffled. "We haven't been fair to Annie."

Taylor shook her head. "Whatever." She walked away.

Julia put her hand on Raisa's shoulder. "She'll be OK."

"Come on team, hustle in!" Coach Garcia said, calling the players to the dugout.

Raisa shook off her tension and ran in. She had a game to play.

* * *

The Jets' pitcher let a fastball fly across the plate. Julia swung hard and connected with the ball. She dropped the bat and raced toward first base.

Raisa, who was already on first, launched herself toward second base. She made it just in time.

Next up to bat was Taylor. She hit the ball far into the outfield and sprinted to first.

Raisa raced past third, then sped for home. Her foot touched the plate.

A few seconds later, Julia crossed home. They gave each other a high five as Taylor came to a stop at third base.

The game continued. Annie's turn at bat brought Taylor home, but the Jets caught Annie as she rounded second base and tagged her out.

At the third inning, the Jets were ahead by two runs.

We can catch up. We can win, Raisa thought. *As long as we keep playing as a team, we'll be fine.*

When Raisa took the mound, she struck out the Jets' first batter. The next batter hit the ball, and Taylor went for the second out, but couldn't get the ball to first base in time.

Coach Garcia signaled Raisa to switch with Annie.

"Remember what we talked about," Raisa told Annie as she came to the mound.

Annie tensed, but Raisa smiled. "Do your best and have fun," she said.

Annie grinned. She managed to strike out one player, but the Jets were the better team. Their next player hit a home run, and so did the two players after that.

At the end of the game, the Tigers had lost 6–4.

Raisa ran up to Annie.

"I'm sorry," Annie said, swiping at her eyes. "I tried really hard."

"Everyone can see that," Raisa told her. She hugged her friend.

Annie looked over at where Taylor and Kaitlyn stood with Julia on the sidelines.

"I'm not sure everyone agrees," Annie said quietly. She stared at Taylor, who had her arms folded across her chest.

"Be proud of yourself," Raisa told her. "Taylor will get over it, I promise."

Just then, Kaitlyn and Julia ran over to them. Taylor trailed behind.

"That was an excellent game, Annie," Julia said.

"That's nice of you," Annie said, "But I don't think that's true."

"It is," Taylor said. "The Jets are one of the best teams in the league. You played awesome. When I started out, I wasn't a great player. It took a lot of work and help from my coach and teammates to get better."

"Really?" Annie asked.

Taylor nodded. "I'm sorry I haven't been a better teammate to you," she said. "I promise I'll try to be better." She looked at Raisa. "It's what's best for the team."

"Thanks," Annie said with a grin.

"Let's go shake hands, then we'll go for ice cream and celebrate," Taylor said. She smiled at everyone. "My treat, for my teammates and my friends!"

Author Bio

Natasha Deen loves stories—exciting ones, scary ones, and especially funny ones! She lives in Edmonton, Alberta, Canada, with her family, where she writes stories for kids of all ages. When she's not writing or visiting schools and libraries, Natasha spends a lot of her time trying to convince her pets that she's the boss of the house.

Illustrator Bio

Katie Wood fell in love with drawing when she was very small. Since graduating from Loughborough University School of Art and Design in 2004, she has been living her dream working as a freelance illustrator. From her studio in Leicester, England, she creates bright, lively illustrations for books and magazines all over the world.

Glossary

anxious (ANGK-shuhs)—afraid or nervous about what may happen

balance (BAL-uhns)—a state in which things occur in equal or proper amounts

championship (CHAM-pee-uhn-ship)—a contest held to determine the best or winning player or team in a sport or game

irritation (ir-uh-TEY-shuhn)—the state of being annoyed, or sore and sensitive

league (leeg)—an association of people or groups with common interests or goals

lineup (LAHYN-uhp)—a list of players taking part in a game

pressure (PRESH-er)—a force or influence that cannot be avoided

reunite (ree-yoo-NAYHT)—to come or bring together again after being apart

stance (stans)—a way of standing

Discussion Questions

1. If you were in Raisa's shoes, how would you have coached Annie? Talk about some things you might have done differently.

2. Do you think Taylor and Julia were being fair when they told Raisa she needed to talk to the coach about Annie? Why or why not?

3. Imagine you are a member of the Tigers and saw your teammates not getting along. What are some of the things you would do to help them?

Writing Prompts

1. Imagine you could go back in time to when Raisa was first learning how to pitch. What do you think her first lesson might have looked like? Do you think she would have been a great pitcher from the start? Write a few paragraphs describing her first lesson.

2. Which position do you think would be the most fun to play in softball? Write a paragraph about why you think that position is the most fun.

3. Can you think of a time you helped someone learn a new task? What was it and how did it go? Write a paragraph detailing the experience and how you helped that person.

More About Softball

Learning these softball terms is sure to make watching and playing the game a lot more fun!

ball—when an umpire calls, "ball," it means that the batter has not swung at the pitch and the pitch has landed outside the strike zone

batter up—how an umpire signals for the next batter to come into the batter's box

batter's box—the rectangular area on either side of home plate on which the batter stands while at bat

center field—the part of the softball outfield between right and left field

infield—the area of a softball field enclosed by the three bases (first, second, and third) and home plate

left field—the part of the outfield to the left, from the perspective of looking out from home plate; also the position of the player defending left field

mound—the slightly elevated ground on which a pitcher stands

on deck—if you're "on deck," it means you are the next person up to bat

outfield—the part of a softball field beyond the infield and between the foul lines; this can also refer to the defensive positions making up right field, center field, and left field, or the players who occupy these positions

right field—the part of the outfield to the right, from the perspective of looking out from home plate; also the position of the player defending right field

strike—a pitched ball that is in the strike zone or is swung at and is not hit fair

strike zone—the area over home plate through which a pitched softball must pass to be called a strike

windmill—the way a pitcher rotates his or her arm for the pitch, spinning his or her arm in a circle, like a windmill